Cock-a-Moo-Moo

For Tony, Amelia, Alexander and Theo – J.D-C.

First published in 2001 by Macmillan Children's Books
A division of Macmillan Publishers Limited
20 New Wharf Road, London N1 9RR
Basingstoke and Oxford
Associated companies throughout the world
www.macmillan.com
This edition produced 2003 for The Book People Ltd,
Hall Wood Avenue, Haydock, St Helens WA11 9UL.

ISBN 0 333 90381 1 (HB)
ISBN 0 333 94753 3 (PB)

1 3 5 7 9 8 6 4 2

A CIP catalogue record for this book is available from the British Library.

Printed in Hong Kong

COCK-A-MOO-MOO!

by Juliet Dallas-Conté

illustrated by Alison Bartlett

TED SMART

Poor Cockerel had forgotten how to crow.

When the sun came up in the morning, he took a deep breath and shouted . . .

"COCK-A-MOO-MOO!"

"That's not right!"
said the cows.
"Only cows go moo."

So he tried again.

"COCK-A

QUACK-QUACK!"

"That's not right!" said the ducks.
"Only ducks go quack."

So he tried again.

"Silly Cockerel!"
said the chickens.
"You're getting it all wrong."

Cockerel was very unhappy. "I'm never going to crow again," he said.

But that night, when all the animals were asleep, Cockerel heard a noise.

Someone was sniffing . . .
and rustling . . . and sneaking
into the hen house! It was a . . .

FOX!

"COCK-A-MOO-MOO!"

shouted Cockerel.

"COCK-A-QUACK-QUACK!

COCK-A-OINK-OINK!

COCK-A-BAA-BAA!"

All the animals woke up!

They came running and
chased the fox away.

"We're saved," clucked the chickens.
"You're a hero!" cried all the animals.
Cockerel was so happy.

"COCK-A-DOODLE-DOO!"

he crowed.

And he never got it wrong again.

ALSO PUBLISHED BY MACMILLAN:

Over in the Grasslands
by Anna Wilson
illustrated by Alison Bartlett

Charlie's Checklist
by Rory S. Lerman
illustrated by Alison Bartlett

 MACMILLAN CHILDREN'S BOOKS